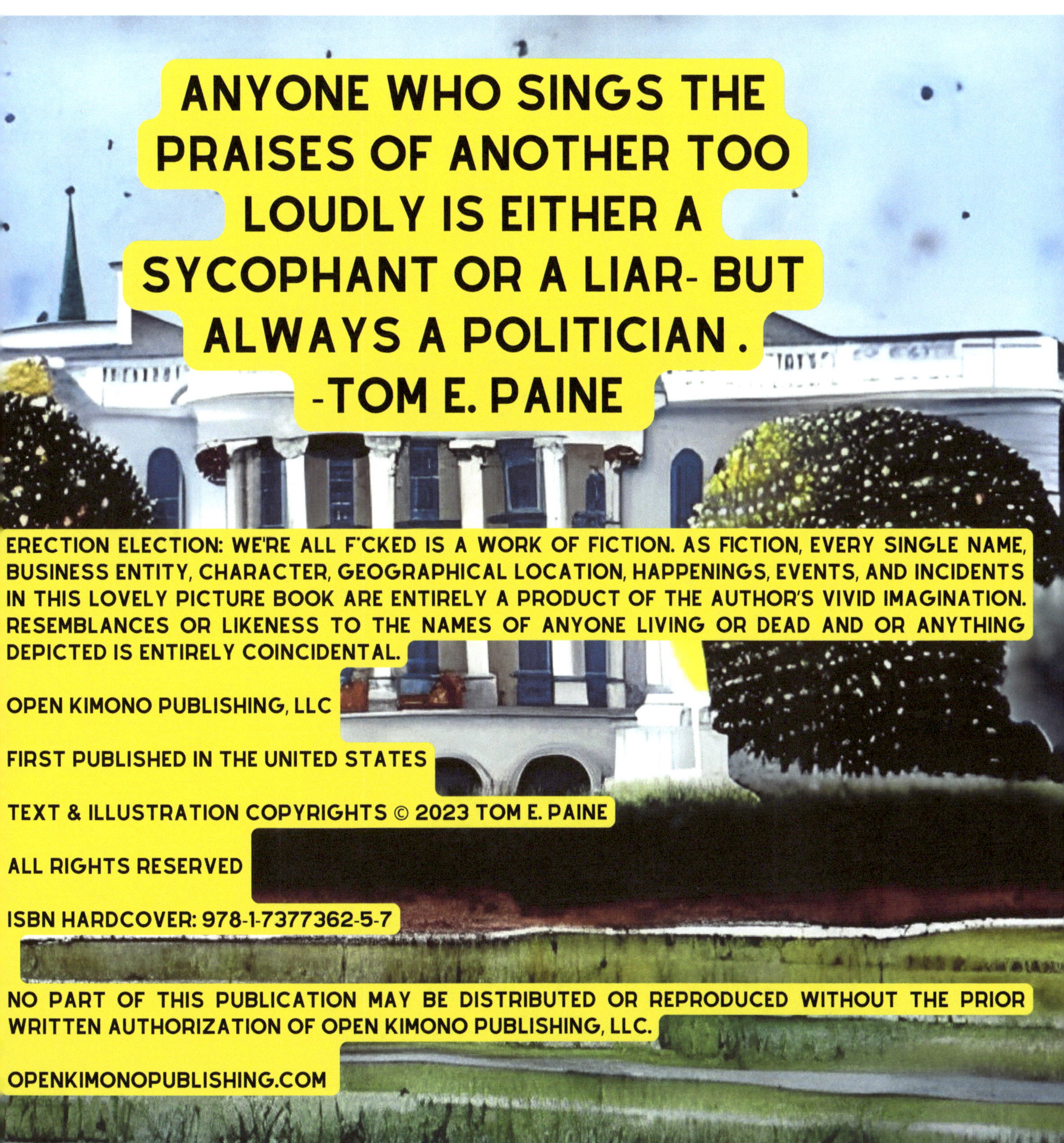

ERECTION ELECTION: WE'RE ALL F*CKED IS A WORK OF FICTION. AS FICTION, EVERY SINGLE NAME, BUSINESS ENTITY, CHARACTER, GEOGRAPHICAL LOCATION, HAPPENINGS, EVENTS, AND INCIDENTS IN THIS LOVELY PICTURE BOOK ARE ENTIRELY A PRODUCT OF THE AUTHOR'S VIVID IMAGINATION. RESEMBLANCES OR LIKENESS TO THE NAMES OF ANYONE LIVING OR DEAD AND OR ANYTHING DEPICTED IS ENTIRELY COINCIDENTAL.

OPEN KIMONO PUBLISHING, LLC

FIRST PUBLISHED IN THE UNITED STATES

OPENKIMONOPUBLISHING.COM

$1,006,849,276.91
BOUGHT ME
THIS OFFICE.

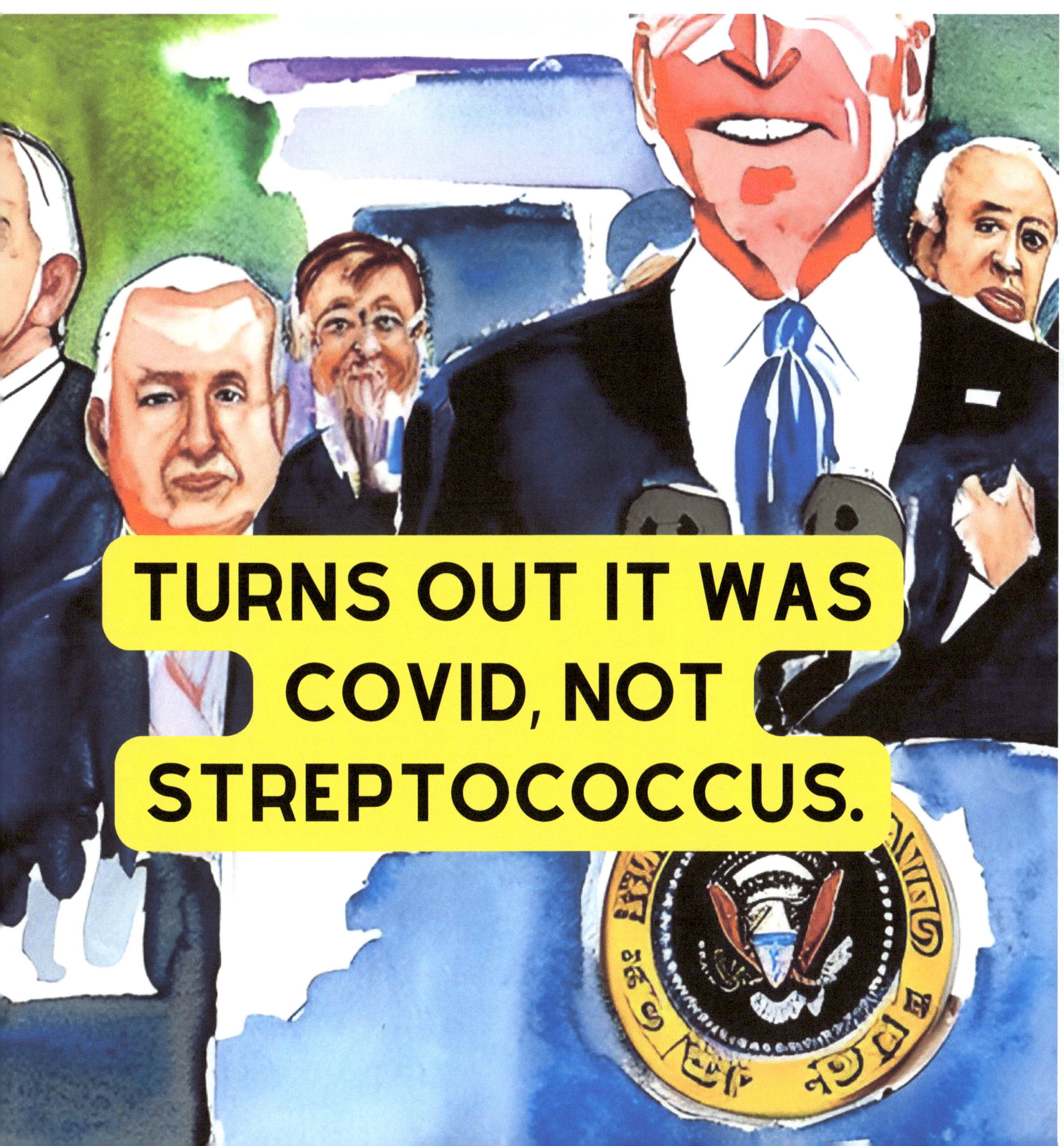

TURNS OUT IT WAS COVID, NOT STREPTOCOCCUS.

THAT MADE THE RIGHT FEEL THE FULL FORCE OF OUR CAUCUS.

MAYBE, IN THE NEXT ELECTION YEAR THEY WONT BE SO CAVALIER IN CLAIMING STOLEN VOTES AND CONDEMNING THE QUEER.

LOOK- 2024 IS NEAR AND REGARDLESS OF THE ELECTION YEAR, CONTROVERSY IS WHAT I SELL. OR MAYBE IT'S FEAR.

I JUST FLEW IN ON MY CUSTOM PJ- Y'ALL HEAR. I'M GOING TO DO MY BEST HERE TO MAKE JESUS AND ALL THE LIBERALS TEAR.

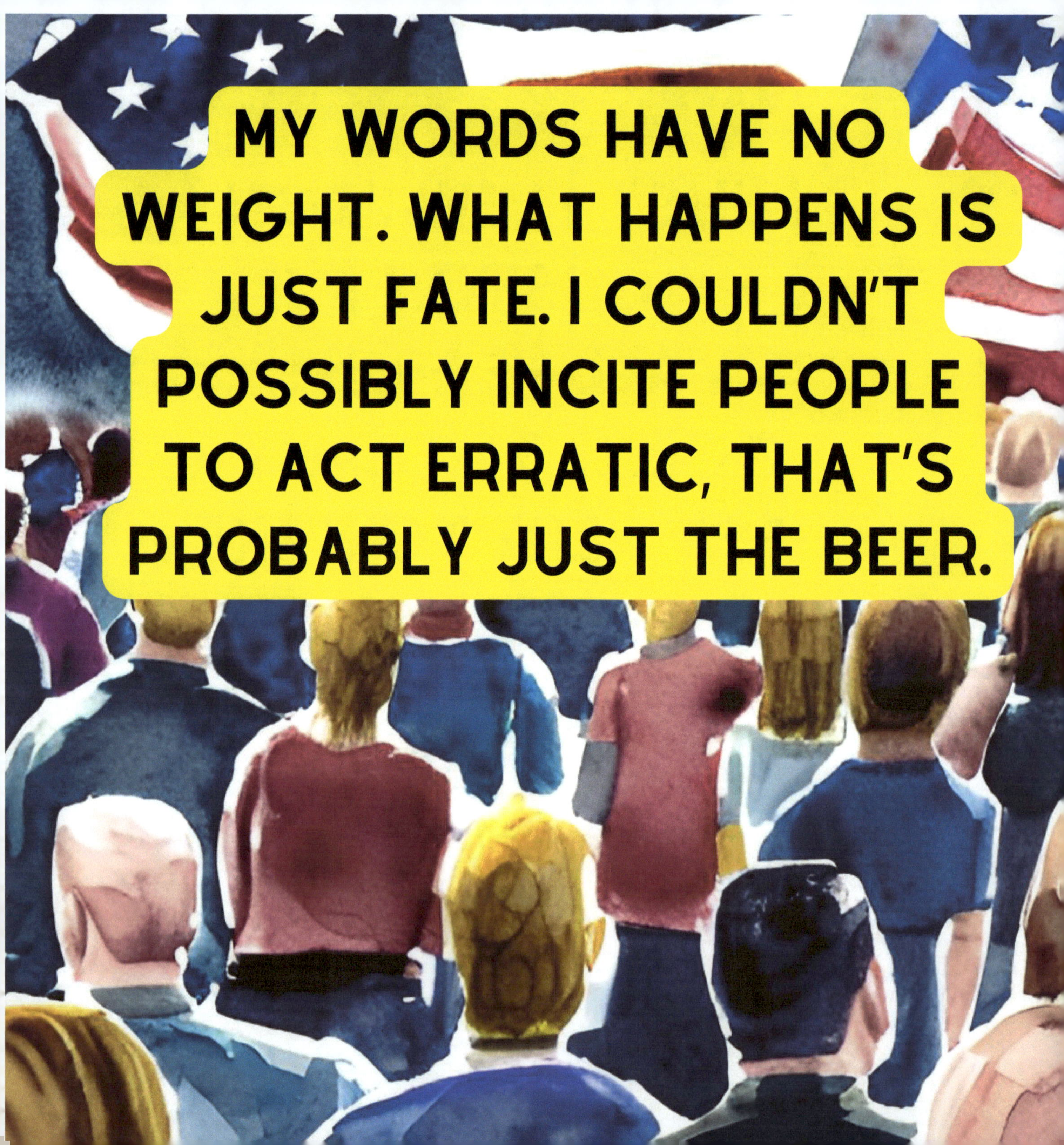
MY WORDS HAVE NO WEIGHT. WHAT HAPPENS IS JUST FATE. I COULDN'T POSSIBLY INCITE PEOPLE TO ACT ERRATIC, THAT'S PROBABLY JUST THE BEER.

BUT LET ME MAKE ONE THING ABUNDANTLY CLEAR. IT'S THE LEFT THAT GOT US HERE.

LOOK, ALL OF OUR PROBLEMS COME FROM THE RIGHT. THEY ARE TRULY THE REASON NONE OF US CAN SLEEP AT NIGHT.

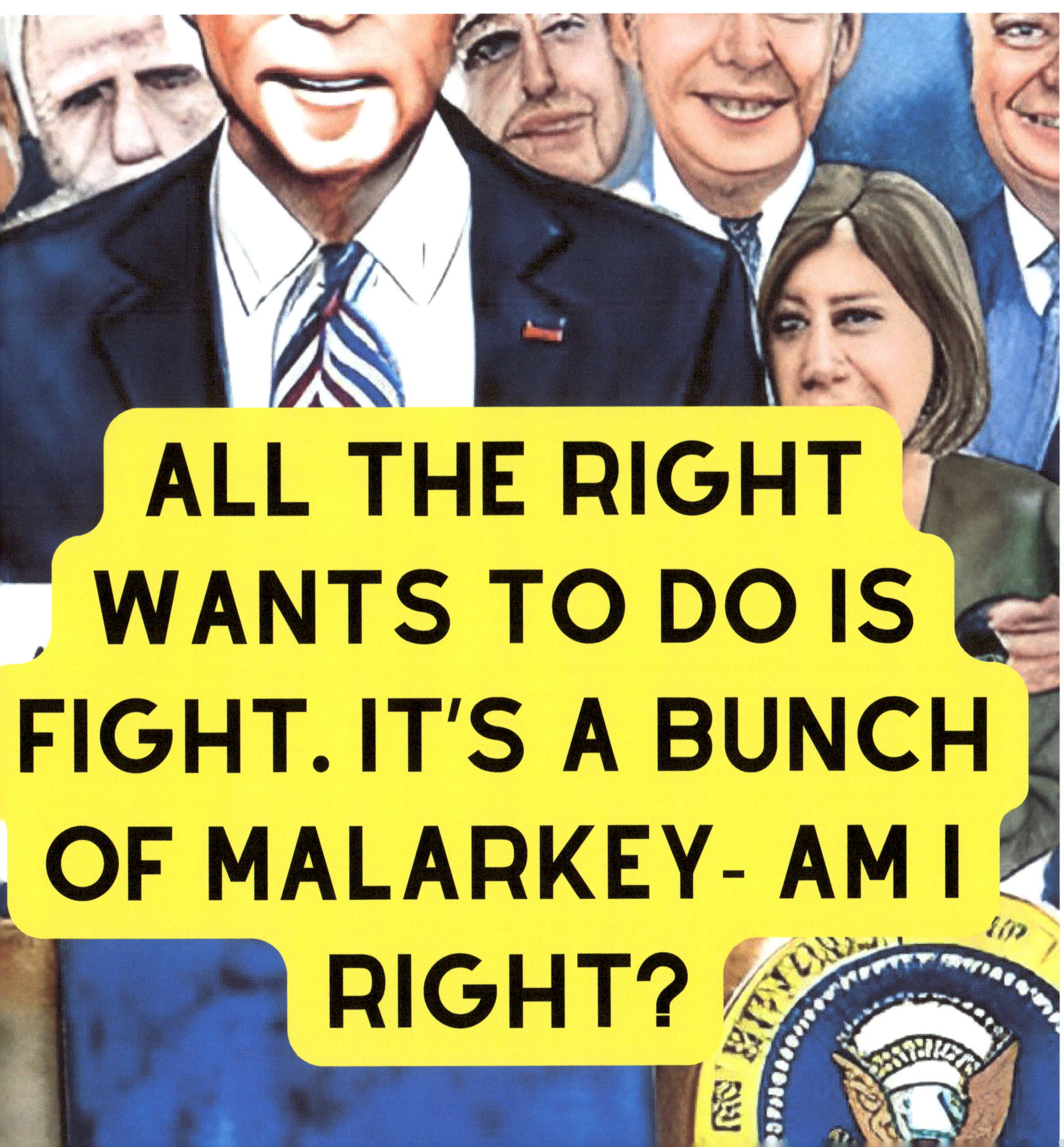

ALL THE RIGHT WANTS TO DO IS FIGHT. IT'S A BUNCH OF MALARKEY- AM I RIGHT?

GRETT
THE RADICAL LEFT IS LEAVING US WITH NOTHING LEFT!

WE NEED TO PUTIN THE WORK IF WE WANT OUR COUNTRY BACK FROM THE LEFT!
RALL

TO HELP PUT THINGS IN OUR FAVOR WE NEED TO SAVOR TODAY, OUR SUCCESSES. DID ANYONE NOTICE THAT SOMEONE INTENTIONALLY LEAKED AN UNPRECEDENTED SUPREME COURT RULING?

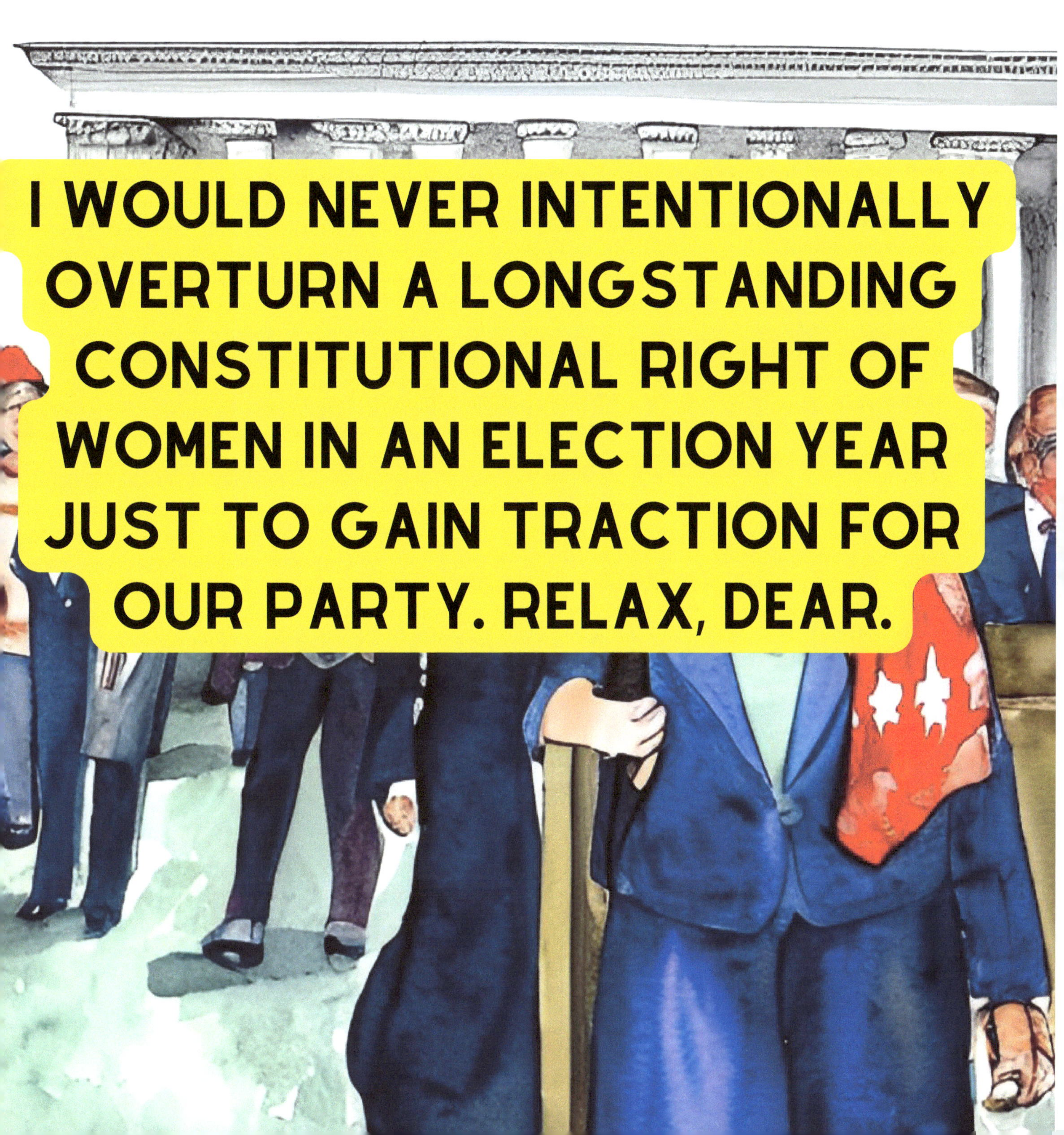
I WOULD NEVER INTENTIONALLY OVERTURN A LONGSTANDING CONSTITUTIONAL RIGHT OF WOMEN IN AN ELECTION YEAR JUST TO GAIN TRACTION FOR OUR PARTY. RELAX, DEAR.

WAIT- DOCUMENTS AT MY HOUSE? IN MY DEFENSE, I DON'T KNOW WHAT'S HAPPENING IN GENERAL, LET ALONE WHAT'S IN MY GARAGE, JUST TO BE CLEAR.

THE DOCUMENTS I HAD WEREN'T CLASSIFIED. I SAID THEY WEREN'T SO THEY'RE NOT. REMEMBER, I'M OUR COUNTRY'S CHEVALIER!

I MUST IMPLORE THAT WE ABHOR THE ACTIONS OF THE RIGHT. I WILL NOT VOLUNTEER ANY OF MY POTENTIAL MISGIVINGS, EVEN IF THEY WERE SEVERE; I WILL NOT FIGHT. GOODNIGHT.

BREAKING NEWS! THE RIGHT AND THE LEFT SQUABBLE IN AN EFFORT TO COMMANDEER OUR NATION'S ATTENTION THROUGH FEAR.
BREAKING NEWS

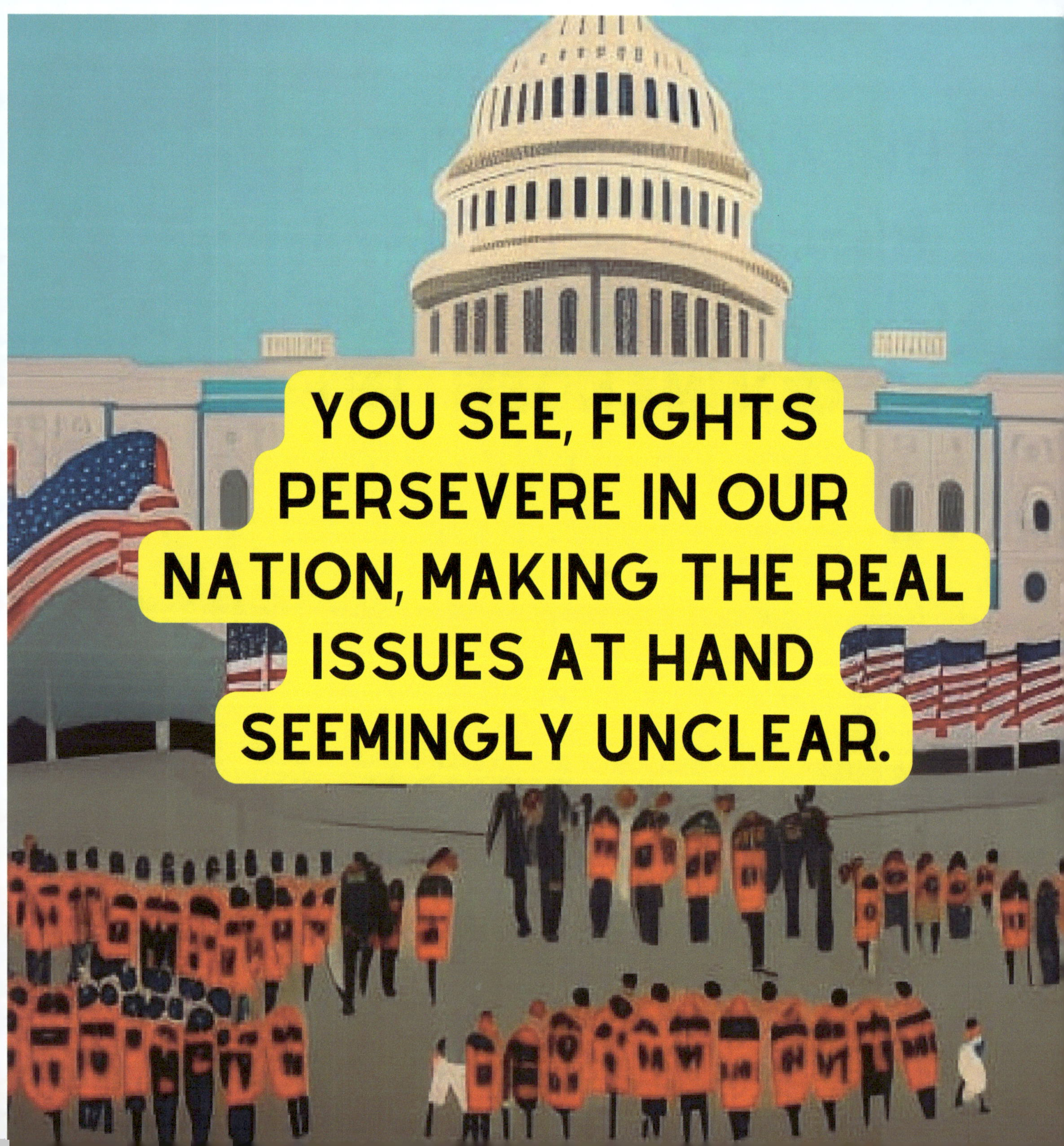
YOU SEE, FIGHTS PERSEVERE IN OUR NATION, MAKING THE REAL ISSUES AT HAND SEEMINGLY UNCLEAR.

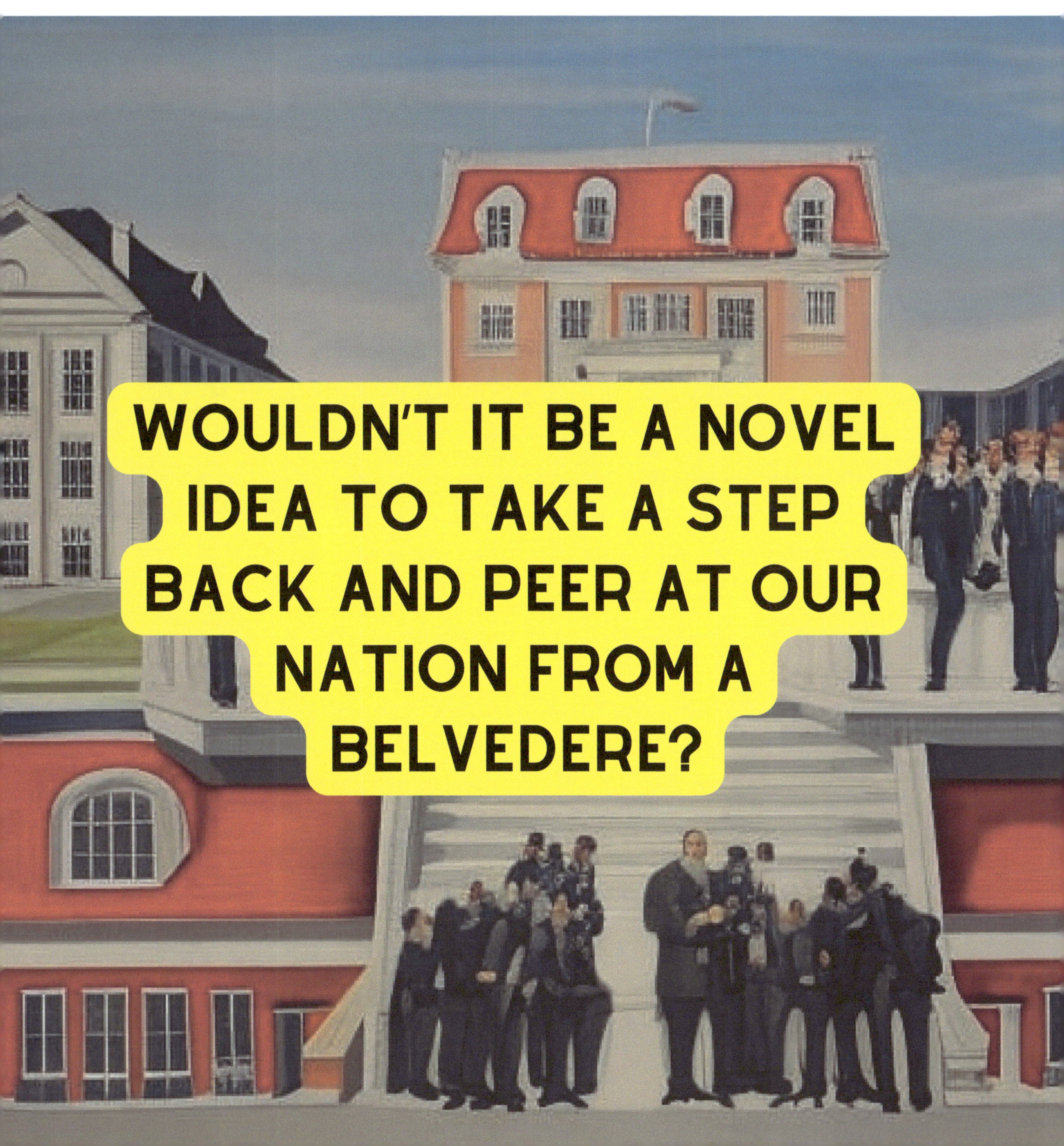
WOULDN'T IT BE A NOVEL IDEA TO TAKE A STEP BACK AND PEER AT OUR NATION FROM A BELVEDERE?

FROM THE TOP WE COULD SEE THAT OUR ISSUES BLEED DOWN NOT UP. OUR REPRESENTATION IS NO MIRROR OF OUR POPULATION.

OUR REPRESENTATION SITS UPON A SLIVER HILL, GLEAMING OH SO PRETTY. FORGETFUL OF THE FACT THAT OUR LIVES ARE SO SHITTY.

HEALTHCARE FOR THEM, FOR US: JUST A CONSPICUOUS OVERPRICED BILL. WHAT A THRILL IT MUST BE TO LOOM OVER US ALL, FROM ATOP CAPITOL HILL.

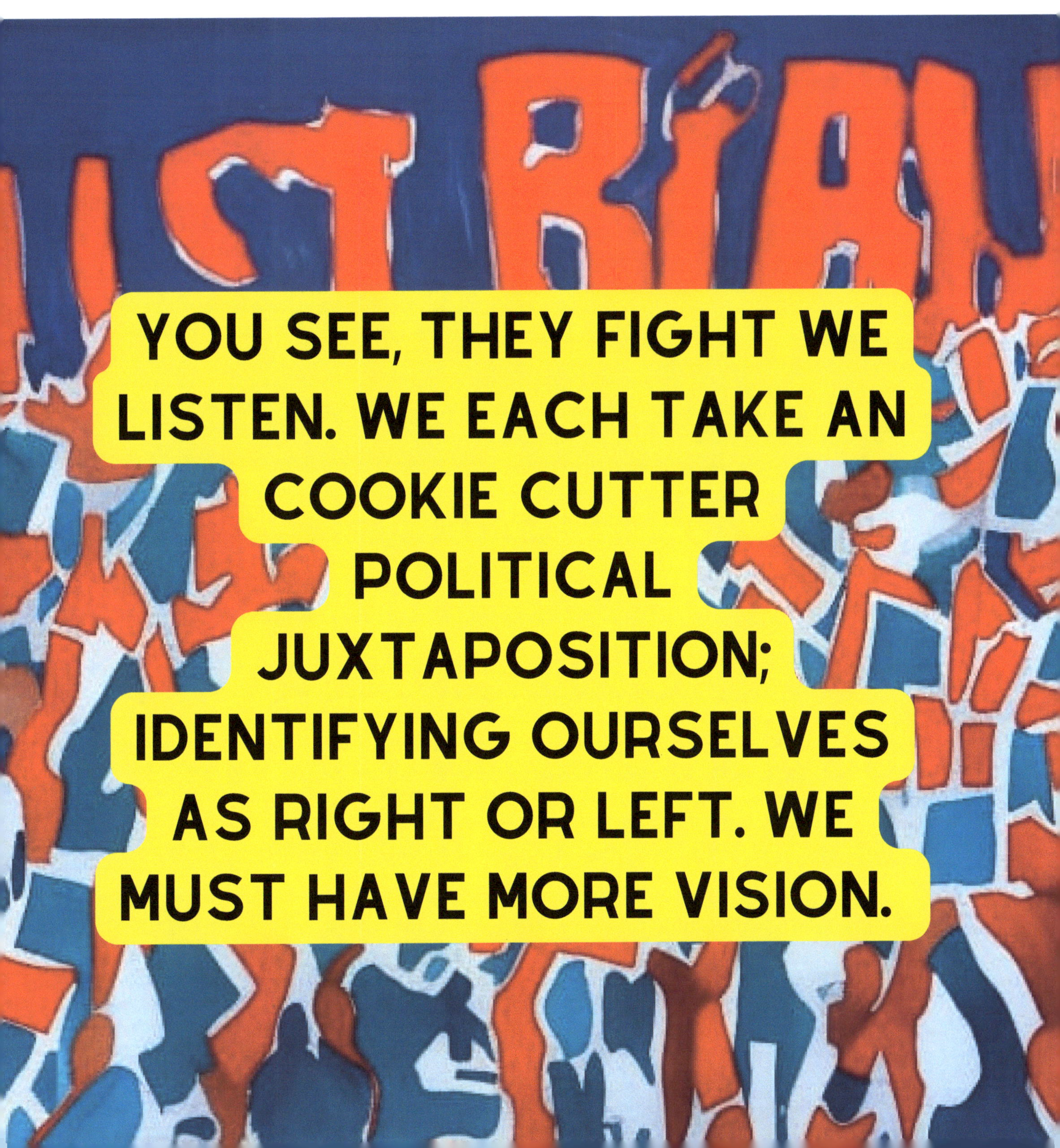
YOU SEE, THEY FIGHT WE LISTEN. WE EACH TAKE AN COOKIE CUTTER POLITICAL JUXTAPOSITION; IDENTIFYING OURSELVES AS RIGHT OR LEFT. WE MUST HAVE MORE VISION.

THE PARTISANSHIP HAS CUT US A BILL WITHOUT A 20 PERCENT TIP. LEAVING US AS A SAIL IN THE WIND WITHOUT A SHIP.

SEE THROUGH THE LIES AND CUT TIES WITH DISCOMBOBULATED PARTISAN THOUGHTS. WE ARE AMERICANS WHO WILL NO LONGER ALLOW OUR COUNTRY TO BE BOUGHT.

OUR NATION IS LOST, UNABLE TO CUT THROUGH THE MORNINGS FROST. MENIAIAL TRIVIALITIES LEAVE US WITH TWISTED THOUGHTS. WE MUST NEVER FORGET THAT OUR THOUGHTS ARE OUR OWN, AS MUCH AS OUR NATION IS ONE. ENOUGH WITH POLITICAL GAMES. WE SHALL SEE THROUGH THE DIRT OF THE THAMES, LOOKING THROUGH CLEAR WATER WE CAN PLAINLY CUT PAST THE FOTTER. WHAT MATTERS IS OUR OWN SONS AND DAUGHTERS. OUR FUTURE IS ONE: TOGETHER. NO MORE INFIGHTING NO MORE POINTLESS PARTISAN SLIGHTING. LET US JOIN TOGETHER, WORK TOGETHER, AND LIVE TOGETHER. TOGETHER WE ARE STRONG. TOGETHER WE CAN CUT THROUGH THE MORNING FOG AND SEE THAT ITS CLEAR WE'RE ALL HERE FOR ONE ANOTHER. WORKING FOR BETTER- A BETTER TOMORROW, WITH LESS SORROW.

www.ingramcontent.com/pod-product-compliance
Lightning Source LLC
Chambersburg PA
CBHW041420300726
48981CB00007B/357